GALLERY BOOKS
An imprint of W.H. Smith Publishers Inc.
112 Madison Avenue
New York, New York 10016

Twin Books

For many years, a wise and good King ruled England well. The people flourished and were very happy.

But by and by, the good King became ill. His captain of the guards was a ruthless, greedy man. He saw the King's weakness as a chance to fatten his own pockets at the people's expense and—worst of all—in the King's name.

It seemed that no one could save the kingdom from the thieving Captain Pete and his ruthless henchmen, until one day . . .

"Kindling! Get your fresh kindling here!" shouted a young peasant boy named Mickey. "You can't cook your dinner without a fire!"

Beside him, his friend Goofy shouted, "Snow cones! Get your snow cones here! Plain and rock and twig! I got all kinds! Get your snow cones! Snow cones!"

But no one on the street stopped. Goofy's shoulders slumped as he said, "Gawrsh, Mickey! If I don't get a customer soon, I'm going to have to eat these myself."

Mickey's dog, Pluto, rubbed up against his master and whimpered. Mickey patted Pluto on the head and said, "I'm hungry, too, boy."

"Come on, gang!" said Mickey. "We've got nowhere to go but up!" He pointed to the King's castle and said, "A little hard work and one day we'll be eating just like them!"

"Really?" said Goofy. "Ice cream and cookies and pie?"

"And ham and potatoes and turkey!" said Mickey. "Lots of turkey!" Pluto licked his chops with a slurp.

The royal coach spun around a corner and spoiled their daydreams with a spray of snow. Pluto snarled as he shook the snow from the point of his nose to the tip of his tail, then sprang after the coach, barking.

"No, Pluto! No!" shouted Mickey.

Pluto chased the coach into the castle, and Mickey had almost caught up when the gate suddenly slammed in his face.

"Pluto. Here, boy," whispered Mickey under the gate.

"Who goes there, and what do you want?" called the guard.

"Uh, I just want to get my dog back," said Mickey.

A window in the gate slid open, and the gatekeeper peered out. When he saw Mickey, he gasped. The weasel threw open the gate and bowed so low, his nose touched the ground.

"Y-Y-Your Highness! Forgive me! Come in, come in!"

Mickey didn't understand what the gatekeeper was talking about, but he thanked him and ran off to look for Pluto.

The gatekeeper was still bowing when a shadow stretched before him. Slowly he raised his eyes and saw a pair of boots that looked just like Captain Pete's. He gulped, raised his eyes a little more and saw a uniform that looked just like Captain Pete's. Then he looked a little higher and saw the face. "Captain Pete!" he squeaked.

"What do you think this is, open house?" said Pete as he grabbed the weasel.

The weasel said, "B-b-but, Captain, that was the Prince!"

"Then who's that?" snarled Pete. The weasel gurgled in confusion as he looked along the line of Pete's pointed finger and saw the Prince sitting by his chamber window.

The Prince slumped in his chair. His teacher, boring old Horace, was lecturing on something-or-other, and how it related to something else. The Prince sneaked glances outside his window at the children playing in the snow.

"Your Highness," said Horace, "please pay attention."

Donald, the Prince's valet, snickered. As Horace went on with his lecture, the Prince pulled out a peashooter and popped Donald twice on the noggin.

"*Wak!*" cried Donald. "Who did that?"

Donald wasn't sure who had shot him, but the Prince looked far too innocent to be innocent. Donald turned, then cried out when he was instantly struck by another pea.

"Donald!" said Horace. "The Prince is trying to study!"

Donald pulled out his own peashooter and fired. The Prince ducked the pea, which sailed over his head and bounced off Horace's backside. Horace turned toward Donald, his face blossoming into an angry shade of purple.

"But he started it!" said Donald as he shuffled out. "Ah, phooey! That stupid Prince always gets me in trouble!"

As he watched Donald leave the room, the Prince snickered. His tutor turned to him and said, "I am very disappointed in you, Your Highness. You know your father is ill and requires rest and quiet."

Suddenly, the Prince wasn't so proud of himself. Horace said, "Now, where were we in the lesson?" But he was cut off by the sound of barking that erupted from the courtyard.

The Prince leaped from his seat, swung open the window and saw Captain Pete clutching a peasant boy and screaming at the boy's dog, "Let go of my leg, ya dumb mutt!"

Down in the courtyard, Mickey struggled, even as a young commanding voice called out, "Captain Pete! What is this uproar?"

"Just some local riffraff, Your Highness!" said Pete.

Then the Prince said, "Even the lowliest subjects of this kingdom deserve respect. Unhand the lad, and apologize. Then have him brought to me at once."

That's when Pete dropped Mickey to the ice-hard ground, bowed low and said, "Sorry . . . punk!" with a false smile. Then a swift kick sped Mickey toward his weasel escort.

Pluto growled, then yipped as Pete tossed him out the castle gate and into a snowbank.

As Mickey walked through the lavish hallway, his eyes drank in the sight of more wealth than he had ever imagined. Crystal and gold glistened everywhere. Even the floor sparkled like the silver surface of a lake.

Mickey was so intent on the riches around him, he stumbled against a suit of armor. The helmet toppled onto his head, while the suit of armor clanged against the armor beside it.

When the Prince rushed out of his chambers, the whole row of armor came crashing down around him.

"What's going on here?" cried the Prince, as a helmet fell on his head.

"Who turned out the lights?" cried Mickey, staggering back and forth as he tugged at the helmet stuck on his head.

The Prince struggled to get his helmet off, too, and tugged and tugged as he tottered across the floor.

When they met in the middle of the hallway, their helmets smashed together like the crash of a great gong. Mickey and the Prince fell to the floor, and got their first glimpses of each other through the openings beneath their visors.

They pulled off their helmets and gasped. Each felt as if he were staring into a mirror that had come to life.

The Prince blinked. "You look . . ."

". . . just like me," said Mickey.

"Who are you," said the Prince, sizing up Mickey, "and who is your tailor?"

"My name's Mickey, Your Highness."

"The beggar boy!" exclaimed the delighted Prince.

"I'm so glad you came!" said the Prince as he escorted Mickey into his chambers. "When you're a prince there's never a moment to yourself. Breakfast and lessons, then lunch. Fencing, tea time, then feasts and banquets and more banquets, day after day after day!"

At the first mention of food, Mickey's mouth had begun to water. He was starving!

"How I envy you your freedom," sighed the Prince. "No homework . . . you play all day and stay up as late as you like! Oh, if I could take your place for just one day."

"That's it!" exclaimed the Prince. "I shall take your place in the streets of London, and you shall be the Prince!"

"B-b-but, I can't be the P-P-Prince!" said Mickey.

The Prince dressed Mickey in some of his clothes and said, "Of course you can. Just walk around saying, 'Guards, seize him!' and no one will know the difference."

"But what would the King say?" asked Mickey.

"He'll never know," said the Prince, with a wink.

It wasn't long before the Prince was wearing Mickey's clothes and sliding down the vine outside the bedroom window. Mickey said, "You won't forget to come back, will you?" But the Prince was already too far away to hear.

The Prince dropped to the ground and glanced gleefully around, with his first taste of real freedom. His freedom didn't last longer than the time it took Captain Pete to snatch him up by the scruff of his neck.

"Peasant boy!" snarled Pete. "You shouldn't have embarrassed me in front of the Prince."

"Peasant boy?" said the Prince, struggling for breath. "My dear Captain, you've made a mistake. I'm the Prince!"

"Oh, really?" said Pete. He set the Prince on a catapult, released the trigger and laughed. "Have a nice ride, Your Highness!"

The Prince went up, up, up, then down, down, down. "*Oof!*" he said as he plowed face-first into a snowbank. He came out sputtering.

Pluto bounded through the snow and gave the Prince a big slurpy lick, then suddenly stopped and sniffed. He sniffed again to be sure the Prince wasn't Mickey, then turned and stomped away.

The Prince didn't know that the dog belonged to Mickey, so he was delighted. He said, "Obviously, my disguise has worked, if even a dog can't recognize royalty when he sniffs it."

"Mickey! Hey, Mickey!" called Goofy, rushing forward.

"My first encounter with the peasantry!" said the Prince.

"Where'd you go, Mickey?" asked Goofy.

"Who's Mickey?" replied the confused Prince.

"You are," said Goofy.

"Oh, yes! You must forgive me," said the Prince. "I'm so dreadful with names. May I please have your name?"

"What's the matter with the one you got?" said Goofy. "*Hyuck!* Don't you remember? I'm Goofy."

"So I see," said the Prince as he backed up, then turned and ran away as fast as he could.

Goofy followed, shouting, "Hey, Mickey! Wait up!"

Pluto just shook his head as he lay down next to the front gate and waited for Mickey to show up.

Mickey sat at the Prince's desk in the royal chambers, drooling over Horace's lecture on the link between the Greek and Latin alphabets. He was so hungry that "alpha, beta and gamma" came out sounding like "sausage, pancakes and potato salad." When Donald rolled the dinner cart into the room, Mickey could barely stand it.

"Constantinople is the capital of what country?" asked Horace.

Mickey stammered, "It's, uh . . .uh, it's . . ." He looked at the giant bird Donald was carving. Mickey could almost taste the—"Turkey!" he said.

"Turkey is correct," said Horace. And that's as far as he got before Mickey bolted for the food.

Mickey didn't even get a grape, much less a taste of turkey, before Donald stopped him and said, "Don't be hasty, Your Highness! Remember, I have to taste it first."

Mickey watched in agony as Donald took a slice of turkey and gobbled it up. "Is it okay?" asked Mickey hopefully.

"Delicious!" said Donald, smacking his lips. "There is no poison on that slice of turkey. But let's see about this slice . . . and that apple. Hmmm, it could be dangerous. The orange, mmm, the salad, the pudding. . . .Yum-yum, this sure is good stuff!"

Mickey couldn't believe that his dinner was being slowly taste-tested away. "I hereby decree," he stammered, "that I, uh, don't need my food tasted anymore!"

"Sorry!" munched Donald. "It's a very important job."

"Just a nibble?" pleaded Mickey, grabbing a drumstick. Donald snatched at the drumstick, shaking his head. But Mickey wouldn't let it go, no matter how hard Donald tugged.

Donald screamed, "I'll report you to the— *Wak*!" He lost his grip and rolled head over heels into the hallway.

Mickey took a bite from the drumstick and said, "Thanks for lunch, Donald!" Then he slammed the door.

"There's something funny about that boy," said Donald.

The day went by very quickly for Mickey and the Prince. While the Prince roamed the streets of London, Mickey was fitted for a new suit of clothes.

When the Prince saw children having a snowball fight, it looked like so much fun that he decided to join them. But he was soon overwhelmed by flying snowballs, and wondered whether this was what "fun" was all about.

Meanwhile, Mickey was learning some of the finer points of falconry, the sport of hunting with falcons. The first thing he learned was how to duck.

Their day went from bad to worse.

The Prince tried to play "fetch the bone" with a cute little dog. But the dog was more interested in playing "fetch the Prince," and the Prince barely escaped with his trousers intact.

KA-
BOO

During his chemistry class, Mickey discovered that when he mixed a little too much of this with with a little too little of that, he got a "*boom!*"—a very big one that blackened everything in sight. Horace was not amused.

Meanwhile, a dozen other dogs had joined in the game of "fetch the Prince."

This day was definitely not going according to plan.

Later, the Prince sighed in relief. The dogs were busy barking up someone else's tree, and he was free to continue his tour of the town. Then he heard a woman cry, "Help! Help me! For the children's sake, won't someone please help me?"

The Prince rushed around a corner and saw a guard and a peasant woman tugging at two ends of a chicken.

"Relax, lady," said the guard. "It's for the King."

"Yeah, the King," snickered another guard.

"But this chicken's all we have!" said the woman.

"Well, then, it's all we'll take," snarled the guard.

The Prince stepped up and said, "As your royal prince, I command you to unhand that hen!"

As the Prince advanced toward the guards, they burst out laughing. The Prince was furious. "What is so amusing?" he demanded. That made them laugh even harder.

One of the guards grabbed a pumpkin and giggled, "Gosh, Your Highness, I didn't recognize you without your crown." Then he crowned the Prince with the pumpkin and snatched the chicken. The two guards stomped away, laughing.

The Prince shouted, "You can't steal in the King's name! When I return to the palace, I'll make you pay for this!"

"They never pay for anything," said a boy who helped the Prince to his feet. The Prince couldn't believe it.

The Prince stood in the snow, shaking his head. How could he be trying to have fun when none of his subjects was happy? Something had to be done! But what?

"Make way, you slugs, for the Royal Provisioner!" The Royal Provisioner wallowed on the seat of his wagon as it rolled down the street, overflowing with stolen food.

The Prince reached into his pouch and pulled out his Royal Ring, the only thing he had brought from the castle. This was the answer! He leaped in front of the wagon, held up the ring and shouted, "Halt! As your prince, I command you to give the food to the people!"

The Provisioner saw the ring and gasped, "the Prince!"

"It's the Prince!" ran the cry through the crowd.

"The Prince! The Prince!" echoed through the street.

Goofy didn't see the Prince anywhere. "You're all goofy!" he said. He remembered that Mickey had been acting strange, too. "Something must be going around. I sure hope I don't catch it," Goofy said to himself. Then he stopped and stared. Was that Mickey standing on top of the royal wagon, throwing out food to the townsfolk?

The Prince handed the peasant woman two chickens and a string of sausage. She said, "Oh, thank you, Your Highness."

Goofy rushed forward, waving his arms. "Hey, Mickey! Get down from there! You're going to get us in trouble!"

"From His Majesty, the King!" said the Prince as he tossed out a ham, which smacked Goofy in the face.

A squad of weasel guards forced their way through the crowd. The Royal Provisioner pointed to the Prince and said, "That's the boy who showed me the ring!"

One of the weasels drew his sword and said, "You're under arrest for impersonating the Prince!"

"And you should be fired for impersonating a guard!" said the Prince, leaping to the ground. With a leg of ham, he parried a thrust of the guard's sword. Though the Prince was quickly surrounded, he fended off their flashing blades as well as he could, until his ham ran out.

Goofy saw that his friend was in trouble and rushed forward to help. But he stumbled across a barrel, slipped, flew into the air and landed in the back of the Provisioner's wagon. The horse was so startled that it bolted across the square.

Meanwhile, the Prince was reduced to protecting himself from the guards with only the short stub of a ham bone.

Suddenly, the wagon smashed through the guards. Goofy lifted the Prince up and carried him to safety.

"Thank you, Goofy!" gasped the astonished prince.

Back at the palace, Captain Pete paced back and forth across his quarters as he listened to the guard. The guard said, "All I know is, the boy acted like a nobleman . . . and he had this!" The guard held up the Prince's Royal Ring.

"So that was the Prince I threw out," said Pete.

"You threw out the Prince?" said the guard with a gulp. "Oh boy, are you ever going to get it!"

Pete grabbed the guard by the collar and sneered, "Not if he doesn't come back alive! We'll see to that, won't we?"

Mickey was completely unaware of the events that were unfolding around him. "Take that! And that!" he said, swinging his sword at an empty suit of armor.

There was a knock at his chamber door as Mickey took one last swipe at the armor and lost his grip on the sword. It sliced Horace's hat in two as he entered the room.

"Nice shot, Your Highness," said Horace. "But I fear the time for games is at an end. Your father is in his last hours and wishes to see you at once."

"There's something I've been meaning to tell you . . . " began Mickey, but he was interrupted by Horace.

"Your Highness, please, time is of the essence."

As Mickey was escorted down the long hallways, he decided to tell the whole story to the King. Once he was inside the King's vast, dark chambers, he took off his hat and advanced slowly toward the bed that was raised high on a platform. "Come closer, my son," whispered the King.

Mickey stepped next to the bed and said, "But . . ."

"From the day you were born," said the King, "I have tried to prepare you for this moment. I shall be gone soon, and you will be King. You must promise me that you will rule the land from your heart, justly and wisely." The King held out his hand and said weakly, "Promise me, my son."

Mickey took the King's hand. "I promise," he said.

Mickey sniffled back tears as he left the King's chambers. The weight of the nation fell on him to find the Prince and tell him the sad news. Then Mickey looked up and saw Pete standing there, flanked by several guards.

"Good day, my phony Prince!" said Pete as he hoisted Mickey by the collar. "Now that our dearly departed King is out of my way, you're going to do every little thing I say, or"—he pulled Pluto from around a corner, yelping—"you may have a dearly departed dog."

"But, but," stammered Mickey, not knowing what to do.

"I'm glad we understand each other," said Pete.

That night, bells rang throughout the town.

When the Prince heard the bells, he rushed to the window of Goofy's room and called out to a man in the street, "You there! What's happened?"

The man called back, "The King is dead, and the Prince is to be crowned at once."

For a moment, the Prince didn't move or say a word as he gripped the windowsill. Then a tear slid down his cheek, and he bowed his head.

"Father!" said the Prince.

As the Prince left the window, Goofy looked up from the dinner pot and said, "Your soup's almost ready, Mickey."

"I can't believe it," said the Prince. "He's gone."

"What are you talking about, Mickey? Who's gone?"

"My father, the King," said the Prince. "And now it's up to me to right the wrongs I've seen: Children going hungry, corruption everywhere . . ."

"Gosh!" said Goofy. "You mean you really are the Prince?" The Prince nodded. Goofy gulped, then knelt and said, "Sire, your wish is my command."

The Prince placed a hand on Goofy's shoulder and said, "Then come, friend. We must return to the palace at once!"

Pete appeared in Goofy's doorway and said, "You will be returning to the castle, my Prince—in chains!" He turned to his weasel guards and said, "Get 'em, boys!"

The guards charged into the cramped quarters and flung their spears. The weapons flew toward the Prince like a swarm of bumblebees, pierced his clothing and pinned him to the floor.

Goofy grabbed a broom and wielded it like a mighty sword. He struck, he slashed, and gave the guards' armor the best cleaning it had ever had. Suddenly, a spear caught Goofy by the collar, yanked him off his feet and carried him out the window. He screamed all the way to the River Thames.

"Drat!" said Pete. "Now he's escaped!"

Pete smuggled the Prince into the palace and up the stairs to a cell. "You'll pay for this!" said the Prince.

"I never pay for anything!" said Pete. "But you should worry more about yourself, because once the pauper is crowned, there'll be one too many Princes around." Then Pete threw the Prince into the cell and slammed the door.

Donald squinted out of the darkness of the dungeon and said, "Your Highness! There's an imposter in the palace."

"I know, Donald," said the Prince as he heard the distant sound of trumpets. "The Coronation has begun, and I'm the one who placed the pauper on the throne!"

The crowd buzzed with excitement as they waited in the Great Hall for the crowning of the young Prince.

Mickey stood in the wings, clutching the curtains, and prayed that the Prince would show up soon. Horace took Mickey gently by the sleeve and said, "We are ready to begin, Sire." Mickey turned and saw Pete standing in an archway with Pluto straining at a leash. Pete smiled a wicked smile while Pluto whined.

Mickey gulped and allowed Horace to escort him down the long aisle.

From the dungeon, the Prince shouted, "Open this door immediately!"

"Ahhh, shut up!" said the guard, standing outside the cell. Then he heard the sound of footsteps, turned and saw the shadow of the executioner stretching up the gray stone steps and stairway walls. "You won't have much longer to wait," he snickered.

The executioner had almost reached the cell when he tripped and knocked the guard unconscious with the flat side of his ax. "Gawrsh! I sure am sorry!" said Goofy as he pulled off his hood.

"Goofy!" cried the Prince.

"Just sit tight, little buddy!" said Goofy as he fumbled for the keys. "I'll have you out in a jiffy!"

Each step toward the throne made Mickey more and more nervous. Where was the Prince? Why didn't he come? So many questions and no one to answer them. The processional trumpets stopped when Mickey reached the throne. The Archbishop stood beside the throne and said, "Be seated, Sire."

"After you," said Mickey, trying to stall.

"Oh, no, beauty before age," said the Archbishop.

"Oh, no, age before beauty," said Mickey.

"Your Highness is such a sport," chuckled the Archbishop. "Sit down!"

"Okay," said Mickey, as he eased onto the throne.

The Prince and Donald strained at the bars of the cell as Goofy tried the first key. It didn't fit frontways, backways, sideways or any other way. "Hyuck!" said Goofy. "You can never be too careful."

The pounding of footsteps echoed up the stairway. "Hurry, Goofy! Hurry!" said the Prince.

"I am hurrying," said Goofy. He held up another key on the ring, then said, "Now I've lost count." He went back to the first key and tried it again.

Suddenly, a dozen guards spilled out of the stairway. Donald screamed, grabbed the keys from Goofy, jammed one into the keyhole and threw open the door!

The Prince, Donald and Goofy sprinted through the tower passageways, trying to escape the guards and their pointed spears. But every time they turned a corner, they saw more guards, more spears and fewer directions to turn.

And then there were no more ways to turn. They were forced to run toward a door at the end of a tunnel, a dozen guards behind them. The Prince reached the door first and swung it open. To his surprise, the door opened high above the outside of the tower. The Prince managed to hang onto the knob, and Donald and Goofy managed to hang onto the Prince. But the guards weren't so lucky. They streamed out of the tower like water from a faucet, fell and splashed far below in the castle courtyard's fountain.

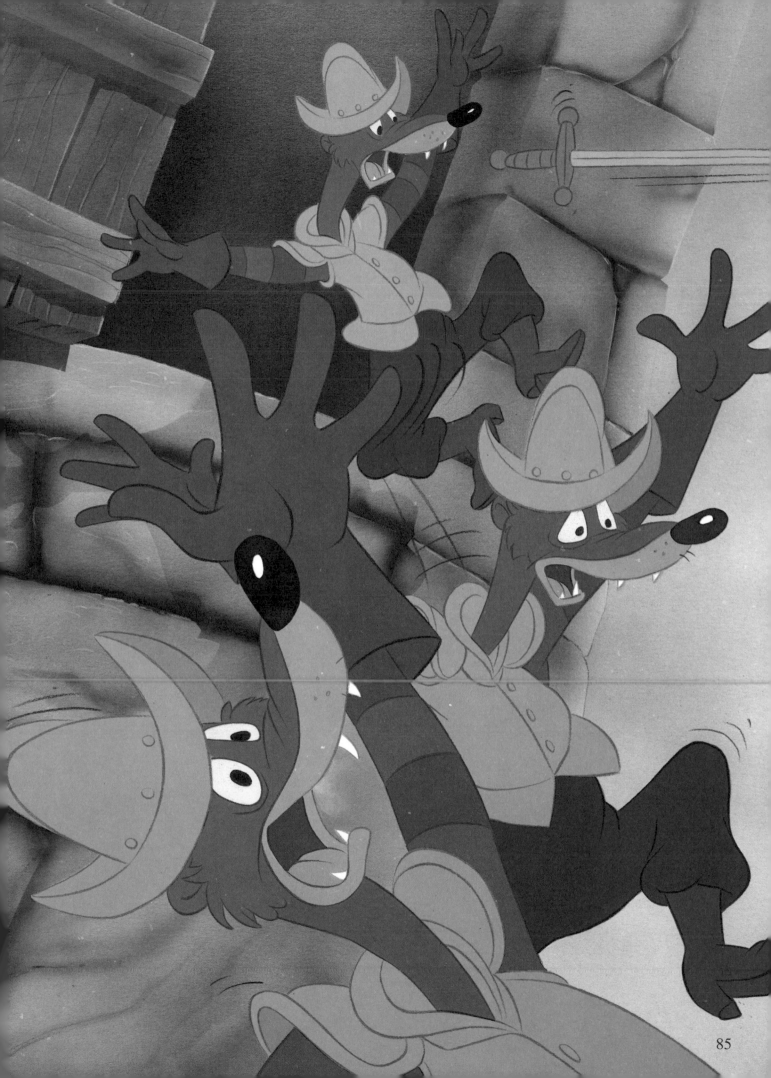

Meanwhile, Mickey searched the Great Hall for any sign of the Prince. All he saw were the expectant, upturned faces of the crowd and Pete edging forward, his face flushed with victory.

The Archbishop lowered the king's crown toward Mickey's brow and said, "It is my honor to crown you . . ."

Mickey squirmed out from under the crown, leapt to his feet and said, "Stop!" The crowd gasped. Mickey said, "Since I'm the Prince, my every order must be obeyed, right?"

"Uh, yes, Sire," said the Archbishop, puzzled.

"Well, then," said Mickey, pointing to Pete, "Captain Pete is a traitor! Guards, seize him!"

"That boy is an imposter!" screamed Pete as he pointed at Mickey, who barely had time to blink before he was surrounded.

"But I'm not!" called out a voice from above.

"Huh? What?" said Pete as he looked up to see the Prince standing in a balcony window. The Prince swung down from a chandelier, snatched a sword from a guardsman and landed at Pete's feet. The Captain was cornered.

"Oh, boy!" said Mickey. Pluto barked in agreement.

"I can explain everything, Your Highness," said Pete.

"Very well," said the Prince. "Explain."

Pete bowed very low, grabbed the edge of the carpet and yanked the carpet out from under the Prince's feet.

Pete charged the fallen prince.

"Hang on, Your Highness!" shouted Goofy, as he leapt from the balcony to the chandelier with Donald grasping his ankles. They swung high over the heads of the crowd. That's when Goofy's fingers slipped.

A guard drew back his bow with an arrow aimed straight for the Prince. Then Goofy and Donald fell on the guard and flattened him to the ground. His arrow flew wide and cut Pluto loose from his leash. Goofy jumped to his feet and grabbed the bow. He reached for an arrow, got Donald instead and accidentally shot the valet into a post on the other side of the room.

Goofy freed Donald from the post and they tumbled backwards, accidentally cutting the rope that held up a chandelier. The chandelier crashed down and trapped a dozen guards in its circle of steel. The crowd cheered!

The Prince and Pete fought furiously, their swords swinging and clanging and ringing and banging. When a guard sneaked up behind the Prince, Mickey laid him low with a blow from the Royal Staff. "Thanks, Mickey!" said the Prince.

"Any time!" said Mickey as they battled back-to-back. Then Pete lunged, and the Prince disarmed him. Suddenly, it was all over.

As the cheering rose to a thunderous roar, Mickey and the Prince embraced at the center of the Great Hall. "Am I glad to see you!" they both said, then laughed.

The Archbishop stepped up, holding the crown. He looked from Mickey to the Prince, then back to Mickey. "How shall I ever know which one of you is which?" he said.

Pluto ran through the crowd and leapt into Mickey's arms. "I guess there's no fooling you, boy!" laughed Mickey between licks. "He's the Prince, and I'm the stand-in."

"In that case," said the Archbishop, placing the crown on the Prince's brow, "I hereby crown you King of England!"

"Long live the King!" cheered the crowd, even louder.

The young King never forgot the lessons he'd learned when
he and the pauper had changed places that fateful day. And
so, with Mickey and Goofy at his side, he ruled his happy
country as he'd sworn he would: with justice and compassion
for all.

Published by Gallery Books
An imprint of W.H. Smith Publishers Inc.
112 Madison Avenue
New York, New York 10016

Produced by Twin Books
15 Sherwood Place
Greenwich, CT 06830 USA

© 1990 The Walt Disney Company

ISBN 0-8317-2433-1

1 2 3 4 5 6 7 8 9 10